463

✓

THE DAY RAVI SMILED

by Gillian Lobel
illustrated by Kim Harley

Tamarind

FOR ALL THE RIDERS, STAFF AND VOLUNTEERS AT PENNIWELLS
G.L.
FOR GLYN AND JOE
K.H.

Published by Tamarind Ltd, 2005
PO Box 52
Northwood
Middx HA6 1UN

Text © Gillian Lobel
Illustrations © Kim Harley
Edited by Simona Sideri

ISBN 1 870516 76 1

Printed in Singapore

Hi, everyone! My name's Joylyn, but I'm usually called just Joy, for short.

Let me tell you something about my week.

Today's Sunday, right, and on Sundays I always go swimming with Mum and Dad and Conor. (He's my little brother, and sometimes he's a real pain in the you-know-what, but mostly he's OK.)

1

On Mondays I go to piano lessons after school.

On Tuesdays it's table tennis at the Leisure Centre.

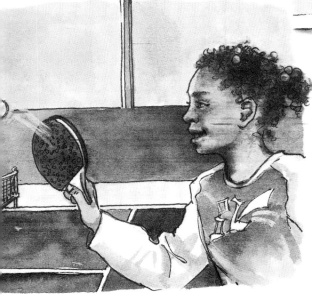

On Wednesdays I go to tea with Alisha – she's my best friend – or she comes to tea with us, and on Thursdays it's Conor's football practice. I always go with Mum and cheer him on. (He's a really brill footballer for such a little kid.)

On Fridays I go to Drama Club. We're doing *Sleeping Beauty,* and I'm the queen. I wear a crown made from gold card, all stuck with jewels – they're plastic but you'd never know! And I sit upon a purple throne…

And on Saturdays it's PENNIWELLS!

Penniwells is a place right out in the countryside, where I go to ride horses. Lots of kids go there, and it's GREAT. There are so many horses and ponies, I'll just tell you about my favourite ones.

First there's Dory. He's quite a small pony, so often the new kids ride him. He's grey and dappled all over. I think the dappled bits look like those high clouds you sometimes see, all speckled and silvery…

Then there's Prince. He looks a bit like Black Beauty – he's black all over, except for this lovely white blaze on his forehead.

My *very favourite* horse is Tyson. His name makes him sound a bit scary, but he's not – he's as gentle as a lamb!

He's the most beautiful horse I have ever seen… He's the colour of a field of corn in the summer, and when the sun shines on him, his coat turns to pure gold. He's got a long silky mane and tail, and they're a sort of milky cream.

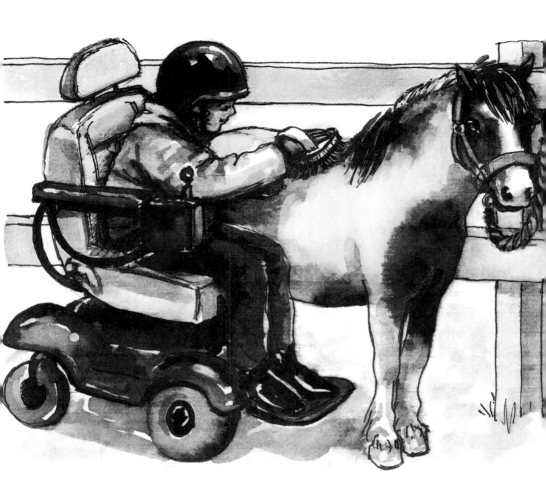

At Penniwells, we're allowed to groom the horses.
I often groom Fluffy. He's a little brown and white
Shetland pony, ever so soft and gentle. I can sit in
my wheelchair and groom him really easily.

Tyson is too tall for me to reach, so I hold his head while one of the helpers grooms him. She brushes and brushes him, till his coat shines like honey.

I take him little treats – he loves apples, and carrots too. Sometimes he turns and nuzzles me with his soft velvety nose.

That's how a horse gives you a kiss. It's tickly and a bit damp and sometimes it makes me laugh. Then he whinnies, in this soft horse voice and blows down my ear.

One day, when I'm grown up, I'm going to have riding stables of my own, and Tyson will be my very first horse…

There's one more horse I really must tell you about. Her name is Missie, and she's a Shetland pony like Fluffy. (I used to think a pony was a baby horse, but that's wrong – ponies are small even when they're grown up.)

And she *is* a character! She's really old – in fact she's a pensioner, like my Grandpa, but she doesn't behave like one!

One day she went missing. Everyone was so worried. How could she have escaped? Penniwells has good strong fences all around, so she couldn't have got out that way – or so we all thought.

Then suddenly, she popped her head over the fence from the field next door. Somehow she'd squeezed under a fence on her tummy!

Now I've told you about the horses, I'll tell you about some of the other kids who go to Penniwells.

There's Emily – she's a really happy, smiley person. She doesn't say a lot, but she loves singing, and she makes up all her own songs. I think that's really cool.

9

Then there's Shem. He uses a wheelchair like me, and he's really good with the horses. He tells lots of jokes, and makes me laugh.

Michael wears special glasses because he can't see very well. He likes to ride Fluffy because he feels safe on him.

He loves to run his hands all over him, and sniff his fur. I know why he likes doing that, because horses have a lovely, warm smell – sort of like honey and biscuits with a bit of leather mixed up in it.

And then there's Ravi.

When I first met Ravi, I just didn't *get* him. You see, he doesn't talk and when you go up to him and say "Hi, Ravi!" – to be friendly – he looks away and waves his hands up and down.

I asked Lucy – she's one of the ladies who look after us at Penniwells – if Ravi couldn't hear. She said he could hear fine but he finds people a bit frightening, and that's why he looks away.

And it's true, he never looks right at you or smiles. When you look at him, he turns his eyes away.

I think eyes hurt him. And it's not just eyes that scare Ravi – he doesn't like doing anything new and he won't ever touch the horses.

Lucy has tried and tried to get him to pat Fluffy or Missie but he gets really upset and starts screaming. Sometimes he just sits in a corner and rocks and rocks.

Then, one Saturday in June something happened...

It was a really hot day – a bit damp and sweaty, if you know what I mean, the sort of day when your clothes stick to you and all you want to do is to splash in a cool swimming pool, and drink lots of lemonade.

But of course it's Penniwells on Saturdays, so heat wave or not, I wasn't going to miss out!

When I saw the horses I could tell they were feeling a bit hot and uncomfortable too. They kept swishing their tails, to brush off the flies.

Dory and Prince always stand head to tail so they can brush the flies off each other's eyes. I love to see them do that.

Anyway, after I'd given Tyson a nice long drink of water, I went to the ramp in my wheelchair and Lucy helped me to mount.

The ramp is dead brilliant, because it brings you right up alongside the horse's back, so if you're in a wheelchair it's ever so easy to get into the saddle.

The moment I'm on horseback I feel so happy – sort of excited and yet calm at the same time. I'm never scared and I want to ride and ride for ever…

Lucy says I have good hands, because I don't tug hard on the reins, and hurt the horses' mouths. I can sort of *feel* what's comfortable for them.

That day Emily was there, and a new boy called Onur, and Shem, and Ravi.

Ravi was having a bad day. I think the heat made him feel cross. He just sat on the balcony that runs round the edge of the indoor school, watching a patch of light dancing on the floor. Sometimes he sits and does that for ages.

I looked at him and wished I could say something to make him feel better – just something to make him smile.

I set off on Tyson, as usual, and Onur went on Dory.

Onur is new, so he had three helpers – one to lead Dory and two to hold him so he felt really safe. That's how we all start.

But I'm a really confident rider, and I go on my own. (I often ride out of doors and last year I went to the Windsor Horse Show with Penniwells.)

We always start off by doing our exercises. These are really important, because they help you keep your balance, and if you're at all stiff, they loosen you up and make you feel great.

We ride with our hands on our hips, or on our heads. That's a bit scary at first, because you're afraid you might fall off – but you don't, because the helpers hold you safe and sound.

Sometimes we swing our arms while we're in the saddle. We practise how to go uphill by leaning back, then we duck down and pretend that we are going through a tunnel.

Onur, the new boy, was really nervous at first. He's very stiff, and he didn't want to do some of the exercises.

Emily loves doing them – she laughs and sings away, and soon she has everyone else laughing too! Even Onur relaxed a bit, but he just wouldn't let go of the saddle!

Lucy said it might rain, so we were riding indoors.

It got hotter and hotter, and there were thunderflies everywhere.

Then it happened. There was this huge peal of thunder.

I don't mind thunder at all, but poor Tyson was terrified. He threw his head up and down and pawed the ground nervously.

"Steady, boy," I said, "Steady." I put my hand gently on his neck to calm him.

Suddenly there was a blinding flash of lightning, and the thunder exploded right overhead.

Tyson reared up in a panic.

Well, you can guess what happened next – I went flying and landed on the floor in the sawdust!

It hurt a bit and for a few seconds I saw stars, but I wasn't scared. I've fallen off before! And I knew Tyson wouldn't hurt me. He calmed down straight away and stood very still.

All the helpers stood really still too, so as not to panic the horses, and then Lucy walked quietly over to help me.

But someone else got there first. Ravi. Before anyone could stop him, he came down from the balcony and trotted over.

He came right up to me and held out his hand. And for a few wonderful seconds he looked right into my eyes. *And he wasn't afraid.*

All the horses knew there had been an accident. They stood very still.

Tyson bent down to nuzzle me. Then he turned to Ravi and gave him a warm soft kiss on his nose. *And Ravi smiled!*

Then he rubbed the horse's nose and said, "Tyson, oh, Tyson!" And he laughed and laughed.

And that was my BEST DAY EVER at Penniwells... the day Ravi smiled.

PENNIWELLS RIDING CENTRE FOR THE DISABLED

was set up in 1980. The centre has just three full time staff and relies on volunteers.

Each week, up to 140 riders come to the school. They have a range of disabilities, from Down's syndrome, cerebral palsy, spina bifida, sight or hearing problems, learning difficulties and behavioural problems.

The stables have 5 horses and 10 ponies, all trained for the special work they do. Everyone is encouraged to ride to the extent of their ability and that can include dressage and jumping as well as lots of fun and games. Also, children learn to look after their ponies.

Among the benefits the children gain from riding are independence, relaxation, balance and co-ordination. They develop a sense of well-being and an increase in confidence.

Edgewarebury Lane
Elstree
Hertfordshire
www. penniwells-disabledriding.co.uk

OTHER TAMARIND TITLES

TAMARIND READERS:
Ferris Fleet the Wheelchair Wizard - NEW
Hurricane

BLACK PROFILE SERIES:
Benjamin Zephaniah
Lord Taylor of Warwick
Dr Samantha Tross
Malorie Blackman
Jim Brathwaite
Baroness Patricia Scotland of Asthal
Chinwe Roy

The Life of Stephen Lawrence

AND FOR YOUNGER READERS
A Safe Place - NEW
Princess Katrina
The Feather
The Bush
Boots for a Bridesmaid
Dizzy's Walk
Zia the Orchestra
Mum's Late
Rainbow House
Starlight
Marty Monster
Jessica
Yohance and the Dinosaurs
Kofi and the Butterflies

www.tamarindbooks.co.uk